In loving memory of this book's talented
creator—our father, Robert M. Lopshire
—Martin, Howard, Terry, and Vicki

Text copyright © 1993 by Robert M. and Selma D. Lopshire

Cover art and interior illustrations copyright © 2020 by Maria Karipidou

All rights reserved. Published in the United States by Random House Children's Books,
a division of Penguin Random House LLC, New York. The text of this book was first published
in the United States by Western Publishing Company, Inc., Racine, Wisconsin,
in a different form, in 1993.

Random House and the colophon and Beginner Books and colophon are registered trademarks
of Penguin Random House LLC.

The Cat in the Hat logo ® and © Dr. Seuss Enterprises, L.P. 1957, renewed 1986.
All rights reserved.

Visit us on the Web!
rhcbooks.com

Educators and librarians, for a variety of teaching tools, visit us at RHTeachersLibrarians.com

Library of Congress Cataloging-in-Publication Data is available upon request.

ISBN 978-0-525-58033-1 (trade) — ISBN 978-0-525-58036-2 (lib. bdg.)
ISBN 978-0-525-58035-5 (ebook)

Printed in the United States of America

10 9 8 7 6 5 4 3 2 1

First Edition

Shut
the
Door!

by Robert Lopshire
illustrated by Maria Karipidou

BEGINNER BOOKS®
A Division of Random House

My mom had gone to town that day,
while I stayed home so I could play.

I played about an hour or more
before I saw that open door.
If Mom saw that, she'd sure be sore.
She always said to shut the door!

I went inside and shut the door.
I saw a fly . . .

. . . and then four more.

And then I saw a lot of flies,
and all of them were on Mom's pies!

I took the pies outside with me
and ran as fast as fast could be.
The flies blew off as 'round I tore,

and then I saw that open door—
as open as it was before.
Those flies could come
and eat some more!

I took the pies and ran inside.

I saw it then . . .

. . . and almost died!

There sat a frog in Mom's best vase,
a silly grin upon his face!

I took the frog outside with me,
back to the pond where he should be.

I also did what I'd done before—
I did not think to shut the door!

I raced my way back home once more—
and saw a skunk go in the door!

A skunk can make an awful stink!
But what to do? I had to think. . . .

And then I knew what I should do.
All skunks love eggs. I'd give her two!

I asked that she go out with me.
She asked for eggs. I gave her three.
But when I had that skunk outside,
I saw the door was open wide!

When would I think to shut that door?
First, flies! A frog! A skunk! What more?

As soon as I got in the door,
I saw some tracks on Mom's clean floor!
Those tracks were like a kind of path
that led me right up to our bath.

I heard a sound—
a "glub, glub, glub!"

I saw a moose there in our tub!

The mess he'd made would make Mom sick!

I told that moose to get out quick!

But he said no, he would not go,
he liked the tub and water so.

I said I knew a better spot
that he was sure to like a lot.

I asked him then to come with me,
to see the place where he should be.

I took him to that pond of ours
and showed him all the lily flowers.

I knew a moose liked lily flowers.
I read it in a book of ours.

Then, while the moose began to eat,
I ran back home to make things neat.

This time, for sure, I shut the door!
I washed the walls and mopped the floor.

And then Mom yelled,
"I'm home for lunch!"

. . . and right behind her came that bunch!
That bunch was back inside once more . . .

. . . 'cause Mom forgot to shut the door!